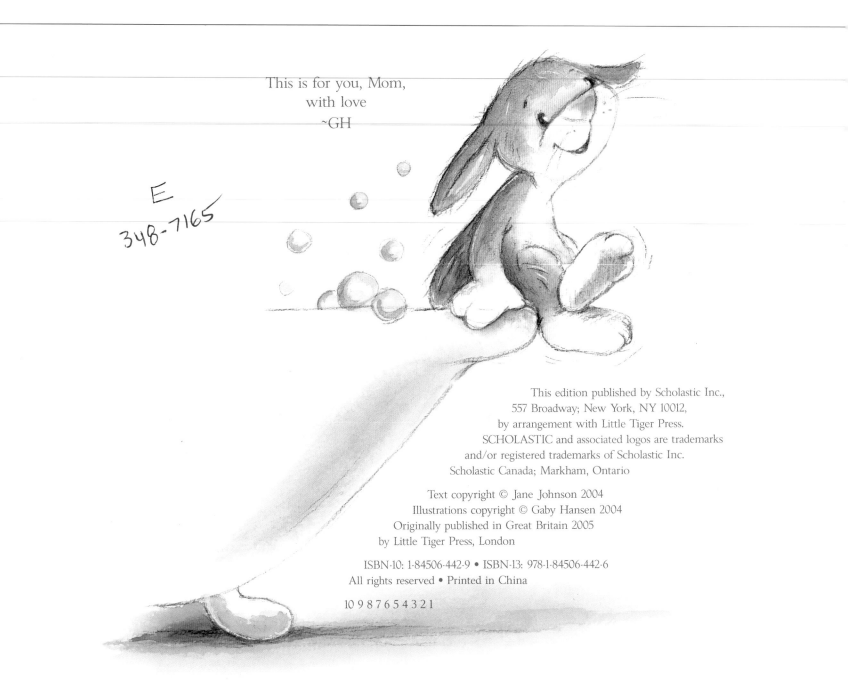

This is for you, Mom,
with love
~GH

This edition published by Scholastic Inc.,
557 Broadway; New York, NY 10012,
by arrangement with Little Tiger Press.
SCHOLASTIC and associated logos are trademarks
and/or registered trademarks of Scholastic Inc.
Scholastic Canada; Markham, Ontario

Text copyright © Jane Johnson 2004
Illustrations copyright © Gaby Hansen 2004
Originally published in Great Britain 2005
by Little Tiger Press, London

ISBN-10: 1-84506-442-9 • ISBN-13: 978-1-84506-442-6
All rights reserved • Printed in China

10 9 8 7 6 5 4 3 2 1

Little Bunny's Bathtime!

Jane Johnson

illustrated by

Gaby Hansen

"Bathtime for my bunnies!"
called Mrs. Rabbit, and her
children all came running.
All except her youngest
little bunny.

"I don't want a bath,"
said Little Bunny.
"I want to go on playing."

"You really want to play all by
yourself?" asked his mommy.
Little Bunny nodded, but
now he wasn't so sure.

"Well, you be good while
I'm busy with the others,"
said Mrs. Rabbit, plopping
them into the water.

"Swish, swash, swoosh," sang
the little rabbits happily, swirling
their bubbles around.

Little Bunny wanted
to play, too.

"Look at me!" he called,
hiding behind the towels.

"Yes, dear," said Mrs. Rabbit, but
she went on washing the others.
"Tickly, wickly, wiggle toes," giggled
her little bunnies, wiggling their
feet in the water.

"Guess where I am?"
shouted Little Bunny,
hidden in the
laundry basket.

"Found you," smiled
his mother, lifting
the lid . . .

But she turned back
to finish washing
the others.

"Up you come!" puffed Mrs. Rabbit,
lifting her children out of the tub.

"Rub-a-dub-dub, you've all had a scrub!"
she laughed. "What lovely clean
bunnies you are!"

Little Bunny was upset.
He wanted his mommy
to notice *him*.

So he
climbed
up . . .

and up—as far
as he could.
But suddenly . . .

. . . SPLASH!

He fell into the bathtub!

"Oh my!" said Mrs. Rabbit, fishing
him out right away.

Little Bunny gazed up at her happily.
"I'm ready for my bath now, Mommy,"
he said, smiling sweetly.

Mrs. Rabbit couldn't
help smiling back.
  "Off you go and play
quietly," she said to
the others.

Then she ran
fresh water and gave
Little Bunny a bath—
all to himself.

"Soapy ears and soapy toes,
soapy little bunny nose!" sang Mrs. Rabbit.
She washed his ears while he fluffed
up some new bubbles.
"I love you, Mommy," said Little Bunny.
"I love you too, darling."

She washed his back while
he played with his boat.
 "You're the best mommy in the
whole world," said Little Bunny.
 "And you're my precious
bunnykin."

She dried his fur
and whiskers, and said,
"Ooh, you smell
so clean and nice!"

And Little Bunny kissed his mommy
and hugged her tight.
"There now, all done," sighed Mrs. Rabbit.
"It's time for bed. Where are my other
little bunnies?"

She found them in the kitchen.
"Oh no! What a mess!" cried
Mrs. Rabbit. "You're dirty again!
You all need *another* bath!"

"Yes," giggled Little Bunny.
"All except me!"